Books by Maurice Dolbier

A Lion in the Woods

A Lion
in the Woods

by MAURICE DOLBIER

With Illustrations

by Robert Henneberger

LITTLE, BROWN AND COMPANY · Boston
Toronto

Published simultaneously in Canada
by Little, Brown & Company (Canada) Limited

PRINTED IN THE UNITED STATES OF AMERICA

U. S. 922787

Contents

A Lion in the Woods

"A Little Job That's Happened to Come Up"

YOUNG TIMOTHY HOPPITT knew that this was going to be a very important day in his life, and everyone and everything else in the woods seemed to know it too. The whistled songs of the birds were brighter than Timothy had ever heard them, and the breeze made the cool green grass bow to him as he loped along on his way to work.

He even saw a four-leafed clover, and ate it, and nothing can be luckier than that.

When he came to the cave with the sign on the door:

THE DAILY BLADE
"All the News We Can Find to Print"
R. REYNARD: EDITOR AND PUBLISHER

and rang the bell, the prickly old porcupine who served as doorkeeper said: "Good morning, Mr. Hoppitt." It was the first time he had ever called Timothy by

name; always before he had greeted him with a grunt.

"It's a beautiful day," said Timothy.

"Well," said the porcupine, squinting up at the blue and cloudless sky, "we might have rain before it's over."

Timothy laughed cheerfully, and hopped past into the interior of the cave. Rain, indeed! Not today! Today he was the Rabbit the Sun Shines On! He reached in his pocket, just to feel again the note he'd received yesterday afternoon. There it was! He didn't need to reread it. The words ran through his head like a merry song: *"See me in the morning. Important. Red Reynard."*

Of course the note did not say what the owner of the newspaper wanted to see Timothy about, but Red Reynard did not believe in wasting words. He knew that Timothy knew.

As Timothy hopped down the hallway, the door marked SPORTS opened, and the sports editor, big, genial Grabble Brown, came lumbering out. He waved his fat paw at Timothy.

"Hi, Tim!" he roared. "Mr. Reynard's been asking for you."

"He has?" said Timothy. "When?"

"Just a few minutes ago. He's in his office now."

"Oh! Thanks, Grabble."

"Good luck!" said the bear.

He winked, and Timothy knew that Grabble knew. Why, probably everybody in the office knew! Jack Ferret, the *Daily Blade's* star reporter, had been helping Timothy with his writing and giving him advice on the newspaper business ever since Timothy had come to the *Blade,* and Jack had said: "If I ever leave this job, I know who'll take my place."

And now Jack had gone to another newspaper, somewhere in Canada, and the *Blade* had no star reporter, and . . . "'See me in the morning. Important. Red Reynard.' Ta-ta-ta-ta-te-tum! Ta-ta-ta-te-tum!"

Timothy came into the big newsroom of the *Daily Blade,* still singing, and Roberta Robin, the pretty young home-decorating editor, who had the desk nearest the door, looked up and trilled:

"Somebody seems to be feeling happy this morning!"

"Seeing you would make anybody happy," Timothy said gallantly, and he bowed.

Roberta giggled and blushed.

"That's sweet. Sweet," she said. "But I think you have another reason for being happy, don't you? Mr. Reynard's been looking for you."

"Thank you, Roberta," said Timothy. "Grabble just told me. I wonder whether I've done something wrong?"

He grinned, and Roberta said "Oh, you!" and he hopped along down the length of the room, nodding to

his friends—Carruther Caw, the music reviewer; Owliver Wise, the book reviewer; Willie Gray, the stout squirrel who was the *Blade's* political reporter. They all looked up from their typewriters and smiled and waved and made V-for-Victory signs.

He came to the door that said RED REYNARD, EDITOR AND PUBLISHER, pushed it open, hopped into the outer office where Mr. Reynard's secretary said, "Mr. Reynard is expecting you," opened the door that said RED REYNARD: PRIVATE, and hopped into the inner office.

Timothy's heart always beat faster when he went through this door, but today it was pounding so hard that he felt sure Red Reynard's sharp ears would hear it.

"Ah, Hoppitt," said Red Reynard, who sat behind the biggest desk in the cave, a desk covered with papers and telephones and books. "Sit down."

"Yes, sir," said Timothy.

"You got my note?"

"Yes, sir."

"Good. Now you may be wondering why I sent for you."

"Well, sir . . ."

"Yes." Red Reynard pursed his lips and looked sharply at Timothy. "Hoppitt," he said, "I've been watching you for some time. You're friendly and sociable and you seem to get along well with everyone in the office."

"I think that I do, Mr. Reynard."

"You do, Hoppitt. I've made it my business to find out. And because you are such a friendly person, I knew I couldn't find a better person to do a little job that's happened to come up."

The great moment was almost here, and now Timothy's heart was making such a disturbance that he was afraid it might just pop up his windpipe.

"Y-yes, sir," he whispered.

"I suppose you realize," Red Reynard went on, "that when Jack Ferret left us, we lost the best reporter we ever had?"

"Oh, yes, sir," agreed Hoppitt. "Jack was a wonderful reporter—"

"And I've had the problem of finding somebody to take his place," said Red Reynard. "It's taken a great deal of hard thinking, but I'm pretty confident that I've made the right choice."

The moment was here. Timothy took a deep, deep breath. . . .

"Hoppitt," said Red Reynard. "I want you to meet the *Daily Blade's* new star reporter, Harry Fox!"

Timothy held his breath, then let it out slowly and turned his head. In his excitement, he had failed to notice that there was a third person in Red Reynard's office—a thin brown fox sitting in a chair near the door.

"Harry," Red Reynard said, "this is Timothy Hoppitt."

Harry Fox did not rise or hold out his paw, but looked Timothy up and down with his small bright eyes and gave Timothy a twisted, mocking smile.

"Hi," he said.

"How do you do," said Timothy dully, feeling as though his heart had now stopped beating altogether.

"Hoppitt," said Red Reynard, "since you're such good friends with everyone in the office, I thought you'd be the best one to take Harry around and introduce him to the staff. He's a sort of distant cousin of mine, so I'll appreciate anything you can do in the way of making him feel more at home."

"Yes, sir," said Timothy, rising slowly. "I understand. I'll be glad to . . ." He swallowed. "Glad to . . . make him feel at home."

"Let's go, then!" said Harry Fox, leaping nimbly to his feet. "Let's get a move on! No need to waste time!"

"That's right," said Red Reynard. "Don't just stand there, Hoppitt! Harry's a live wire. He's anxious to get to work."

"Right this way, Mr. Fox," said Timothy, holding the door.

Carruther Caw was writing a review of last night's concert, using the hunt-and-peck system on his typewriter.

"Carruther," said Timothy, "I'd like to introduce you to our new star reporter, Harry Fox. Harry, this is Carruther Caw, our music critic."

"Haw," said Carruther.

"Very pleased to meet you," said Harry Fox. "I've always enjoyed reading your reviews, Mr. Caw. They're brilliant and, what's more, they're fair."

"Well," said Carruther, in a pleased way. "Thank you, Mr. Fox. It's very kind of you to say so."

As Timothy and Harry Fox moved away, Harry said under his breath:

"Can you imagine that?A crow writing about music! It's like hiring me to protect a henhouse! And what a homely bird he is!"

Owliver Wise looked up over a book which he was holding close to his eyes.

"Our new star reporter, Harry Fox," said Timothy. "This is our book reviewer, Owliver Wise."

Owliver at first looked astonished, then blinked at Timothy sympathetically.

"This is a great pleasure for me," said Harry Fox. "I've always enjoyed reading your reviews, Mr. Wise. They're brilliant and, what's more, they're fair."

"Very nice of you to say so," said Owliver, with a modest lowering of his fat old feathered head. "Such compliments are always most agreeable."

As Timothy and Harry Fox moved away, Harry muttered:

"Books! I've never read a book in my life, but I'm smarter than he is. The world'd be better off if there weren't any books. And what a stupid face he has!"

"This isn't Willie Gray?" said Harry Fox, in an awed voice. "Not *the* Willie Gray?"

"Yes," said Timothy. "Willie, this is our new star reporter, Harry Fox."

"Our new . . ." Willie began. He stopped and glanced quickly at Timothy. "Oh?"

"Why," said Harry, "you don't know how I've looked forward to meeting you. Everybody agrees that you're the best political reporter in the business."

"They do?" said Willie.

"Yes, indeed," said Harry. "It's a great honor for me to shake your paw."

As Timothy and Harry Fox moved away, Harry wiped his paw on his coat and said:

"Politics! Why, I know more about politics than he ever will! If I didn't have this job, I wouldn't mind taking over his. I could write rings around him. And what a fat stomach he has!"

"Willie Gray is my best friend!" Timothy exploded. "And I won't have any sly, slinking creature come in here and say—"

"What are you going to do?" Harry grinned, showing his teeth.

Timothy didn't answer. He led the way to a big desk near the center of the room, with an empty chair before it and a covered typewriter on it.

"This is your place," he said, and turned away.

"Hold on a minute!" said Harry. "You're supposed to introduce me to the whole staff."

"No need to waste time," said Timothy. "I have work to do."

"If you're looking for work," Harry said, "you can begin by changing the ribbon in my typewriter. Then you can get some paper for me and sharpen up a few pencils."

"That's a job for copy boys."

"I thought you were a copy boy."

"I'm a reporter," said Timothy firmly.

Harry Fox grinned again.

"You'd better show me more respect, or maybe," he said, "one of these days you'll find that you're a copy boy after all."

2

"Suppose
It Wasn't
Supposing"

EARLY IN THE EVENING a few months later, Timothy was returning to the office to write a news story for the next day's edition when he heard a heavy shout behind him. He turned and saw Grabble Brown.

"Going to work?" said Grabble. "So am I. May as well walk along together."

"Yes," said Timothy.

And as they walked they talked about what every reporter on the *Daily Blade* had been talking about ever since Harry Fox arrived. They talked about Harry Fox.

"I don't like him," said Grabble, "and I don't trust him. But he has a nose for news."

"I don't trust him," said Timothy, "and I don't like him. But he knows the forest inside and out."

"He has a crooked mind, if you ask me," said Grabble. "But's he's fast on his feet, and he's always on the spot when a big story happens."

"He's always saying what a great writer he is," said Timothy. "But the worst part of it is, he's right."

"Oh, I don't know about that," Grabble grunted. "He's a good writer, but I wouldn't say he was a great one. You can write as well as Harry Fox does, any day in the week."

"Do you really think so?" asked Timothy.

"Of course I do."

"I wish Red Reynard thought so," said Timothy. "I wish he'd give me a chance to show what I could do. With a real news story, that is. But it seems as though . . ."

He shook his head, and they walked on silently until they came to the cave.

It seems as though, Timothy Hoppitt thought as he sat at his desk, looking at the story he had just finished writing—it seems as though since Harry Fox came here to work, the news I've been sent out to report on has been getting less and less exciting. He twitched his pink nose unhappily. This news, for instance:

> The Ladies' Social and Literary Club of Forest Park met yesterday afternoon for a poetry recital and informal musicale at the home of Mrs. Bunny Leaper.
> The hostess read her latest poem, entitled "My Love Is Like a Lettuce Leaf," and Miss Euphemia Sniffing offered a group of three songs, accompanied at the harmonica by Mrs. Sandra Skittish.

Timothy knew that this story would be hidden somewhere on the inside pages of the morning newspaper, and that the only persons who would read it—perhaps the only persons who would find it—would be the members of the Ladies' Social and Literary Club of Forest Park. No one would know who wrote it, but why should anyone care?

"Copy!" he called in a loud squeak.

When Harry Fox shouted this word, the three eager young beavers who served the *Daily Blade* as copy boys always came running to his desk, each one anxious to be the first to take the story from Harry and carry it with speed to Red Reynard. They had done the same for Jack Ferret.

"COPY!" Timothy called again.

One of the young beavers, who sat on chairs near the entrance of the room, looked slowly over in Timothy's direction, pretending that he thought he had heard something, and then looked quickly back at his comic book, pretending that he had been mistaken. The other two did not even open their eyes.

"COPY!" yelled Timothy.

The first young beaver put his comic book down carefully, got up, sauntered to Timothy's desk, took the story, and sauntered to Red Reynard's office.

"Just wait!" Timothy thought. "It won't always be like this. Someday I'll write a story that everyone will read, a story that will not only be on the front page of the newspaper but that will have over it the biggest headlines the *Daily Blade* has in stock. And there'll be a line—a by-line—that will let everyone know who wrote the story."

Idly he picked up a sheet of paper and put it in his typewriter. Dreamily he ran his paw over the keys. Almost without knowing what he was writing, he tapped out one word:

By

And then, becoming more daring, he pushed down the key at the lower left-hand edge of the typewriter, the key called the shift lock that made all the letters big ones, and tapped out two words:

TIMOTHY HOPPITT

So that was what it would look like! He had never seen it before. It looked good to him:

By
TIMOTHY HOPPITT

A by-line!

But what would Timothy Hoppitt write if a really big story came his way? What would a really big story be? Well, just suppose that there was a lion in the woods!

The thought came so swiftly and was so frightening that Timothy couldn't help shivering and looking over his shoulder. Then he said to himself:

"I'm just supposing."

For a moment he felt relieved, but soon a serious look came into his eyes. He thought:

"Suppose it wasn't supposing. Suppose there really was a real lion in the woods and Red Reynard sent you out to get the story. What would you do? Would you say 'Oh, no, thank you, Mr. Reynard! I'd much rather you assigned somebody else'? Or would you say 'Yes, sir!' and go out and get the biggest, most exciting news story this paper ever had? Would you be a reporter—or a rabbit?"

He straightened his back and began to type rapidly:

Jungle terror [he wrote] has come to Forest Park!

At 5:28 P.M. a lion, described as a "huge, ferocious-appearing beast," was seen entering the woods near Eagle Rock.

The animal is said to have come from Highway 47, and may have escaped from the Henneberger Circus, which is giving performances in the nearby village of Seven Corners.

All residents of Forest Park are warned to be on the lookout for this dangerous invader, and to report any knowledge they may have as to the lion's whereabouts to police headquarters or to this paper.

Ten things to do if you meet a lion:

Timothy stopped, frowned, and then crossed out the last paragraph with a line of *x*'s. He could think of only one thing to do if you met a lion: get away as fast as you can.

He read what he had written. It could have been better; Jack Ferret would have pointed out a number of things that were wrong with it. But Jack had always said that news stories should be clear and calm and carry all the necessary information, and that the opening sentence should capture the reader's attention. All these conditions Timothy thought he had met.

"Nearly through for the day?"

Timothy looked up quickly. Willie Gray had spoken.

"Yes, I guess so," said Timothy.

"So am I," Willie said, and yawned. "Home is going to look mighty good to me after hanging around City Hall all day. Have an acorn?"

"No, thanks," said Timothy. "I went to a tea and we had carrot-cakes. I'm not very hungry."

He got up and picked up his briefcase. Then he and Willie started for the door.

"Hoppitt!" a sharp voice barked.

Timothy almost dropped his briefcase. He turned. Red Reynard was standing outside his office.

"Yes, Mr. Reynard?" Timothy said shakily. He started back.

"You needn't come back!" said Red Reynard, in a loud and ringing voice. "I can tell you from here. You were ten minutes late this morning. Don't let that happen again!"

"N-n-no, sir," said Timothy. He felt that everyone in the office was watching and listening, and his ears felt bigger than usual, and pink, and very hot.

"Okay," said Red Reynard. "That's all."

"Y-y-yes, sir," said Timothy. "G-g-good-night, sir."

But the editor had already gone into his office and slammed the door. A copy boy giggled. Timothy's ears were hotter. He and Willie went out.

Willie thought it would be kinder not to mention this little scene, so he said only:

"Not much news today, was there?"

"No," said Timothy. "No, there wasn't."

"It's too bad," said Willie, "that somebody doesn't do something to break the monotony."

A whole night was to pass before he and Timothy found out that somebody had.

3

"I'm Giving You the Story of a Lifetime"

WHEN TIMOTHY ARRIVED at the office next day, he saw by the clock on the wall that he was fifteen minutes early. Feeling quite pleased with himself, he was on his way to his desk when:

"Hoppitt!"

An angry bark from Red Reynard. What could be the matter now?

"Yes, sir?"

"Come into my office."

Timothy obediently followed Red Reynard through the outer office and into the private office. The editor flung himself down in his chair and fired a fierce glance at Timothy from under his bristling red eyebrows.

"Hoppitt," said Red Reynard. "What kind of a reporter do you think you are?"

Timothy thought that he was a pretty good reporter, but he didn't think he'd better say so at the moment, because Red Reynard plainly didn't think anything of the sort. Besides, Red Reynard wasn't expecting an answer. He was going right on in a voice that grew more biting with each word.

"Hoppitt, I've been in this newspaper business for a long time, cub and fox, and in all my experience I have never come across such a stupid, silly, sorry excuse for a reporter as you are."

"Me?" said Timothy.

"Yes, you!" Red Reynard roared. "When the biggest

news story this forest has ever had falls right into your lap, what do you do with it? Do you realize that it *is* big news? You do not! Do you know what you do?"

By this time Timothy was so bewildered that he felt he must be dreaming. He heard himself saying in a dreamlike voice:

"What do I do?"

"Nothing!" Red Reynard snapped. He jumped up and began to prowl rapidly around the office, stopping every now and then to point an accusing paw at Timothy. "That's what you do—nothing at all! You write a story and then you forget that you've written it. Do you send it to me? You do not! You just leave it in your typewriter and go home. And if we didn't have copy boys on this newspaper who know what a big story is, better than you do, it might be in your typewriter still. News can't wait, Hoppitt. Don't you know that? *News can't wait!*"

Now Timothy was beginning to realize that all this was not a dream at all. It was something worse. Much worse.

"Wh-wh-what story are you talking about, sir?" he asked.

Red Reynard came to a halt in back of his desk and glared at Timothy.

"There you are!" he said scornfully. "I suppose you've forgotten all about it. What story, he says! Why, *this* story, of course!"

And he shook the morning newspaper at Timothy, a newspaper whose front page used the biggest headline the *Daily Blade* had in stock, a headline that read:

LION IN THE WOODS

Timothy almost choked.

"But this is . . . ." he said. "But you don't . . . . But how did . . . But . . . But . . ."

"Do you remember now?" Red Reynard asked, with a mean sweetness in his voice. "Is everything beginning to come back to you now?"

Timothy took the newspaper. There was no by-line (he was thankful for that!) but the first sentence was the same:

Jungle terror has come to Forest Park!

He couldn't read any more. He blinked hard, and swallowed, and said:

"But this isn't true!"

"What?"

"It isn't true, any of it. It's just something I made up. I made it up out of my own head."

"Let's leave your head out of this," said Red Reynard. "I could think of a good many things to say about it, but I won't. Suppose you just explain to me what you mean when you say that this story isn't true."

"It's make-believe," said Timothy desperately. "I wrote it because—" Suddenly deciding that this was not the time to explain his reasons for writing it, he went on quickly: "There's no lion in the woods. Really, there isn't."

"Ha!" said Red Reynard.

"This is only . . . only a story I was writing . . . for my own . . . my own amusement. That's all it is."

"Ha!" said Red Reynard. "Ha! Only a story, eh? No lion in the woods, eh?"

"That's right, sir."

"Then what about all the persons who've seen it?"

"Seen it?"

With a single sweep of his paw, Red Reynard pointed to all five telephones on his desk.

"Those telephones," he said, "have been ringing all morning. Ever since the paper came out. At least twenty-five persons have seen the lion."

"But that's impossible!" Timothy protested. "They couldn't have. There's no lion to see."

"Hoppitt," said Red Reynard, "I don't know what you're talking about, and I don't think you do, either. I do know that we're running a newspaper and that our job is to report the news."

"This isn't news!" Timothy squeaked. "It's nonsense!"

"Are you trying to tell me that you know more about news than I do?"

"Oh, no, sir!"

"Are you trying to tell me that this community is made up of dishonest persons who would say that they had seen a lion if they hadn't?"

"No, sir, not dishonest. But—"

"All right, then!"

One of Red Reynard's telephones rang. He snatched it up and barked:

"Reynard speaking . . . Who? . . . Oh, yes, Willie. . . . He did? . . . When? . . . I see. . . . Yes. . . . Yes. . . . You bet!"

He slammed the telephone down and strode from the room. Timothy heard him shouting to somebody in the newsroom:

"Willie Gray is on my line, calling from City Hall. Have the call transferred to your phone and take down his story. Get it in shape fast. We're going to bring out an extra edition!"

He came back to his desk.

"Do you know what's happened, Hoppitt?" he said.

"Mayor O'Possum has just declared that Forest Park is in a state of emergency. That's what's happened! And you're still going to stand there and tell me that there's no lion in the woods?"

"Yes, there isn't—" Timothy began.

Red Reynard stopped him.

"That's enough!" he said, picking up some slips of paper and thrusting them toward Timothy. "Now stop talking and get busy!"

"Busy, sir?"

"Yes, busy, sir!" Red Reynard repeated. "This is your assignment, Hoppitt—your job. You don't deserve it— as a matter of fact, I gave it to Harry Fox but he said he wasn't feeling well and I let him go home. . . . I *would* lose my best reporter at a time like this—just my luck!" For a moment, he seemed to have forgotten that Timothy was there, but he pulled himself together and said sternly: "Hoppitt! I'm giving you the story of a lifetime! You'd better not let me or the *Daily Blade* down!"

"No, sir," said Timothy feebly.

"These are the names and the addresses of all the persons who've called this office and reported seeing the

lion. I want you to go and see each of them, get all the facts you can, and be quick about it!"

Timothy took the slips of paper.

"Facts?" he said. "About—"

"That's it!"

Timothy sighed.

"Yes, sir," he said.

"And if you should happen to run into this lion your-self . . ."

"Sir?"

Red Reynard gave Timothy a one-sided smile.

"You'd better not tell him that you made him up out of your own head! That's all!"

4

"It Smelled Like
Ozone and Old Clover"

THE FIRST ADDRESS on the list was 28 Pine Cone
Avenue, and the first person Timothy saw was a Mr.
Griswold Grunter, an elderly woodchuck whom he
found in the back yard, chucking wood.

"See a lion?" said Mr. Grunter, seating himself com-
fortably on a stump and lighting a very strong pipe.

"Yessirree! I sure did see a lion! Plain as the nose on your face! Yessirree, bob!" And he blew a cloud of blue smoke straight at the nose on Timothy's face.

"Where did you see it, sir?" asked Timothy, twitching his nose and holding his pencil ready over his notebook.

"Last night," said Mr. Grunter. "On my way home from work about midnight I was coming along by Oakdale Road. It was so dark you couldn't see your paw in front of you. Then all of a sudden I saw it!"

"Your paw?" said Timothy.

"No! Nosirree, bob! The lion!"

"But if it was so dark —" said Timothy.

"Now, see here, young fellow!" said Mr. Grunter. "Are you implying that I didn't see a lion over there on Oakdale Road just as plain as the nose on your face?"

"No, Mr. Grunter, but you just said—"

"I said I saw a lion, and I did! I saw its eyes shining there in the dark! Two big shining eyes, two big shining yellow eyes, glaring at me!"

"You saw the lion's eyes. You mean you didn't see the rest of him?"

Mr. Grunter grunted.

"I saw as much as I wanted to see, young fellow! I didn't stay around to see any more. I got away from that neighborhood as fast as I could leg it. Nobody can say I'm a coward, mind you. But nobody can say I'm a fool, either."

"Then . . . I hope you won't mind my asking you this question, sir, but how could you be sure that the eyes you saw were those of a lion?"

"I'll tell you how I can be sure!" said Mr. Grunter loudly. "It says so right in your newspaper, doesn't it?"

At the next address, 543 Beechnut Street, Timothy saw a young lady squirrel, who was so talkative and so excitable that once Timothy had told her who he was and why he had come it seemed as though she would never give him a chance to say anything else:

"Oh, yes!" she chattered. "Yes, come right in quickly and close the door—is it tight shut? I've kept this tree locked up ever since I read the dreadful news! Isn't it dreadful news? A lion, of all things! I think you must be terribly, terribly brave to go out in the woods on a day like this. I wouldn't stir out of this tree for anything, not for all the walnuts in Idaho. Have you seen the lion yet? It must be a dreadful sight—just dreadful! I've never seen a lion, of course, but I can just imagine—"

Timothy pricked up his ears.

"I beg your pardon," he broke in, "but did I understand you to say that you had never seen a lion?"

"Yes," said the lady squirrel. "But I can just imagine! All those teeth! And all those claws—it must be dreadful!"

"You telephoned the newspaper this morning, didn't you?" Timothy went on quickly. "Didn't you report seeing a lion?"

"Oh, no!" said the lady squirrel. "I didn't see the lion—I don't know what I'd do if I should ever actually see a lion. I just couldn't stand it, I know. No, I heard the lion."

"Heard the lion," said Timothy, writing in his notebook. "Now, where did you hear it, and when?"

"Please!" said the lady squirrel. "Please don't confuse me. Just remember that I'm only a home maker and I'm not used to being interviewed for the newspaper. . . . Of all things! Do you suppose they'll want my picture for the front page? I don't take a very good picture—at least, all my girl friends tell me I'm much better-looking than my pictures. But my right profile is better than my left, and perhaps . . . Oh, but you asked me something, didn't you? Now what was it you asked me? I'm so upset!"

"Where did you hear the lion?" Timothy asked patiently.

"Well, the sound seemed to come from over in that direction," said the lady squirrel, pointing with her right paw. "But it could have come from over in that direction," and she pointed with her left paw. "It was a dreadful sound, and I was so frightened that I couldn't be sure. But I think it came from over there," and she pointed with her right paw again.

"And at what time did you hear this sound?"

"Oh, I didn't take any notice of the time. I just ran and hid under the bed until the lion had stopped roaring."

"I see," said Timothy. A thought occurred to him. "Have you ever heard a lion roar before?"

"Gracious, no!" she exclaimed. "And I hope I never do again!"

"Then . . . I hope you won't mind my asking you this question, miss, but how could you be sure that the sound you heard was that of a lion roaring?"

"*Well,*" said the lady squirrel. She looked at Timothy with some annoyance. "I just know it was, that's all. Besides, there *is* a lion in the woods! The newspaper says so!"

At 87 Fern Drive, Timothy talked with the next persons on his list, a Young Skunk and a Younger Skunk, while a Youngest Skunk sat wide-eyed in a corner, listening.

"Seven o'clock this morning," said the Young Skunk. "Bright and early. Coming through Checkerberry Lane. My brothers and me."

"I," said the Younger Skunk.

"What?"

"My brothers and I."

"You needn't get uppity!" said the Young Skunk. "Just because you had the chance to go to school while I have to work hard all day to make a home for us! You needn't get so persnickety!"

"Er . . . the lion?" Timothy suggested. "You saw the lion in Checkerberry Lane?"

"I'm coming to that," said the Young Skunk. "We were coming through Checkerberry Lane, my brothers and . . . and I . . . and just about when we reached the corner of Blueberry Alley—"

"It was after we'd passed the corner," said the Younger Skunk. "And it was about seven-thirty, I'd say."

"You'd say!" the Young Skunk exclaimed. "You'd say! Well, *I'm* saying! I'm the one who's telling this story!"

"You don't have to tell it all wrong," said the Younger Skunk.

"I'm not telling it all wrong!" said the Young Skunk. "You're the one who's wrong. You're wrong lots of times, even if you did have the chance to get an education while I —"

"There's no need to get excited," said the Younger Skunk, moving away a little.

"No," Timothy said anxiously. "Please don't get excited. I'm sure that we can—"

"All right," said the Young Skunk. "Where was I?" Timothy consulted his notebook.

"You had just about reached the corner of Blueberry Alley," he reminded him.

"We'd passed it," said the Young Skunk. "We'd gone way past it. It was about . . . about seven-thirty when all of a sudden I smelled a lion!"

"So did I!" said the Younger Skunk.

"You smelled a lion?" said Timothy, writing this down. "What did it smell like? Can you describe it?"

"It smelled like a lion," said the Young Skunk. "What would you expect it to smell like? It smelled like . . ." He sniffed the air as though trying to recall the odor. "It smelled like ozone and old clover."

"Oh, no!" said the Younger Skunk, shaking his head. "Nothing of the sort. It was more like fishbones and a forest fire."

"A lion smelling like fishbones?" said the Young Skunk indignantly. He turned to Timothy. "Did you ever hear such a crazy thing?"

"It's no crazier than a lion smelling like ozone,"

said the Younger Skunk. He, too, appealed to Timothy: "Is it?"

"I really don't know," said Timothy. "You see, I've never smelled a lion, so I couldn't say."

"Neither have I," said the Young Skunk. "But I know it doesn't smell like a forest fire."

"Nor I," said the Younger Skunk. "But nobody with any sense would say that it smelled like old clover!"

Timothy put his notebook away and his pencil behind his ear.

"You mean to say," he asked, "that neither of you have ever smelled a lion before?"

"That's right," said the Young Skunk and the Younger Skunk together, and the Young Skunk added, "Where would we have smelled a lion?"

"Then . . . I do hope you won't mind my asking you this question, and I do hope that you don't get excited . . . but how could you be sure that the smell you smelled was a lion smell?"

"Be SURE?" the Young Skunk repeated angrily.

"Because!" the Younger Skunk shouted.

"Besides," the Youngest Skunk squeaked.

Timothy and the others looked with surprise at the Youngest Skunk, who was nodding his head and dancing up and down.

"Besides what?" said the Young Skunk.

"Besides," said the Youngest Skunk, "I saw the lion!"

"You saw him?"

"Yes, sir! Sure thing! Oh, my!" said the Youngest Skunk.

Timothy took the pencil from behind his ear and opened his notebook again.

"What did it look like?" he asked.

"Oh, it was terrible!" said the Youngest Skunk. He had stopped dancing, his eyes were wider than ever, and the words tumbled out of his mouth eagerly. "It was the most very terriblest thing you ever saw! It was big as the moon, and it had smoke coming out of its nose, and it had big black and yellow stripes, and . . . and . . . a long, gray, waving trunk!"

Timothy, who had started to write, stopped with a sigh, thanked the skunks politely for being so helpful, and went on his way.

Two hours later he sat down on the bank of Bouncing Brook and went over the notes he had taken during the morning. As he read them, he reflected grimly that he wasn't the only person in the woods who had been making up lions out of his own head.

Mr. Grunter had seen the lion's eyes at midnight on Oakdale Road, but a chipmunk had seen the lion's eyes, also at midnight, on Juniper Drive, which was five miles away.

Several persons had heard the lion roar, but nobody could say any more exactly than the lady squirrel from which direction the sound had come.

Several persons had seen the lion's pawprints, but when they went to point them out to Timothy, the marks had mysteriously disappeared.

Some persons had seen the lion's tail flickering through the thickets; some persons had seen the lion's paws lurking in the leaves.

But nobody had really seen the whole lion. Nobody, that is, unless you counted the Youngest Skunk, and Timothy thought that, on the whole, it was better not to count him.

Timothy scratched his right ear in great perplexity. What kind of news story could he make out of these reports? If he went back to the office and showed them to Red Reynard and said "Don't these prove, sir, that there really is no lion in the woods?" he knew that Red Reynard still would not believe him.

He would think that Timothy was a worse reporter than he had suspected in the first place, and that Timothy had either asked the wrong questions or had made mistakes in writing down the answers.

How much more agreeable it would be if Timothy could blame somebody else for the predicament he was in! If, for instance, he could blame the copy boy who had taken the story out of his typewriter. But Timothy, sitting there on the bank of the brook and staring at his swaying reflection in the water, knew that he could blame only himself. Envy and pride, that was it. He was so proud of his writing and so envious of Harry Fox for getting all the big news stories.

"You thought you could be as good a reporter as Harry Fox, did you?" he said to his reflection. The reflection nodded. "Well, are you?" he asked. The reflection shook its head sadly. "Here you are with a story," he went on, "and you don't have the least notion what to do with it, do you?" A fish jumped, and the reflection broke into a hundred pieces.

Timothy stood up, and swallowed hard. There was only one thing to do now, and he must not let false pride stand in his way. He must go to Harry Fox's home, tell him everything that had happened, and ask for his advice.

5 "A Fine Sense of the Public Interest"

SEVERAL MINUTES PASSED before Harry Fox answered Timothy's knock, and when he did open the door cautiously he did not look pleased at seeing a visitor. He had his left paw in a sling, he had a bandage around his head, and he had a thermometer in his mouth. Taking the thermometer out, he snarled:

"What do you want?"

"I'm sorry to disturb you, Mr. Fox," said Timothy. "Mr. Reynard told me you weren't feeling well, but—"

"But here you are anyway!" said Harry Fox. "Well, come in. Come in! I don't want to leave the door open." He was staring past Timothy's head and his eyes seemed to flicker nervously. "Might catch a chill."

Timothy stepped into the den and Harry slammed the door shut, and bolted it.

"Sit down," said Harry, pointing to a chair by the table in the center of the room.

Timothy sat down. He noticed that the table held a number of bottles of medicine and half a dozen boxes of pills.

"My!" he said. "I didn't realize that you were as sick as this!"

"Just overwork, I guess," said Harry, with a shrug.

"Overwork?" said Timothy wonderingly. "But your arm?"

"Strained my finger on a typewriter key," said Harry. "Writing too hard. Never mind that. What do you want? Reynard send you to find out how I am?"

"Oh, no," said Timothy. "He doesn't know I'm here.

I came because . . . well, because I need your help. You see, there's quite an emergency."

"I know," said Harry. "The lion. That's emergency enough. Come to think of it, I'm surprised to see you out in the woods on a day like this. Aren't you afraid the lion will catch you?"

"No," said Timothy. "I'm not afraid of that at all."

Harry scowled at him.

"Don't try to make yourself out to be braver than everybody else!" he said. "If there's anything I dislike about a rabbit more than that he's a rabbit, it's when he pretends to be brave."

"This has nothing to do with bravery," said Timothy. "I'm not afraid of the lion, because I happen to know that there isn't any lion to be afraid of."

"There isn't any . . ." Harry Fox blinked. "Listen, Hoppitt, it sounds to me as though you might have a fever, too. You'd better see a doctor. No lion? Why, the whole front page of the *Daily Blade*—"

"I know," said Timothy. "That's why I said there was an emergency. I made the lion story up out of my own head, just for fun, and I happened to leave it in my typewriter, and after I'd gone home one of the copy boys saw it and thought it was a real story and took it to Mr. Reynard. And Mr. Reynard printed it."

Harry Fox had been listening to Timothy with his mouth open. Now he began to grin.

"You mean," he said, "the story was a fake?"

"Yes," said Timothy, "but when I tried to tell Mr. Reynard this morning—"

Harry's grin grew and grew until it seemed to spread from one of his thin pointed ears to the other. He chuckled and almost choked.

"Well, if that isn't rich!" he chortled. "The richest thing I ever heard! You know, Hoppitt, I never had much respect for rabbits— I guess I've shown that— never knew a rabbit with a sense of humor, for one thing. But I give you credit. I never heard anything so funny in my whole life!"

And he put his head back and howled with laughter. Timothy moved uncomfortably in his chair.

"Funny?" he said. "I don't know . . . it's pretty serious, isn't it? I mean, printing something that isn't so, and especially something like this that might start a panic?"

Harry Fox quickly changed his expression.

"Yes," he said, "I see what you mean, of course. That shows a fine sense of responsibility in you, Hoppitt, a fine sense of the public interest. You did the right thing in coming to me."

"But what am I to do next?" Timothy asked. "Mr. Reynard won't believe me if—"

"Don't worry about a thing," said Harry cheerfully. He ripped the bandage from his head. "I know how to handle old Red." He took his paw out of the sling. "By the way, you haven't told anybody else about this?"

"Oh, no," said Timothy.

"That's good. The less that's known about it, the better. Because it wouldn't look so well for either you or the newspaper if it got about, would it? No, don't you worry about a thing! You come along back to the office with me. I'll handle old Red."

"But," said Timothy doubtfully, "if you're not feeling well—"

"Oh, I feel fine now," said Harry. "You know, when there's a real job to be done, and you realize you're the only one who can do it, you can't let a cold in the head, or a general run-down condition, stand in your way. Come on!"

"You're sure you feel able to?"

"Never felt better!" said Harry.

He unbolted and opened the door of his den, and as Timothy stepped out Harry gave him such a friendly and unexpected slap on the back that Timothy, once he had caught his breath again, decided that he had never felt better, either, and he didn't worry about a thing.

He didn't worry when, as they entered the newsroom of the *Daily Blade*, Harry whispered in his ear:

"You just go to your desk, Tim, my boy. It'll be better if I see old Red alone."

He didn't worry when, sitting at his desk, he looked up and saw Harry going into Red Reynard's office.

He did worry a little when, ten minutes later, Red Reynard came out and barked:

"Hoppitt, I want to see you!"

But Harry, leaving the office as Timothy went in, gave him a meaningful wink, and whispered:

"Everything's okay!"

To Timothy's relief and surprise, Red Reynard didn't say a word about the lion. He just wanted Timothy to write a short feature article on the anniversary of the Forest Park Human-Watching Society.

Freed from worry and full of gratitude for Harry Fox's kindness, Timothy Hoppitt got a good night's sleep.

In the morning, he woke refreshed and happy. As he hopped through the woods, he hummed a little tune.

He was still humming when he entered the news-room (five minutes early), but when he picked up the newspaper, the tune faded away.

In headlines as large as those of the day before, the *Daily Blade* was shouting:

LION DANGER GROWS! MAY BE TWO!

Beneath this was a by-line :

By
The Blade's Star Reporter
HARRY FOX

And beneath this was a story that Timothy Hoppitt read with growing anger and dismay.

In the most colorful and thrilling words, Harry Fox had written from the notes that Timothy had given him —the notes that proved there was no lion—a news story that strongly hinted there were two lions.

Harry Fox was at his desk, leaning back in a chair and also reading the paper. Timothy hopped swiftly over to him, and stuttered when he started to speak:

"Th-th-th-this!" he said. "Wh-wh-wh-what—"

Harry glanced up with a shadow of annoyance on his sharp face.

"Oh," he said, "it's you, Hoppitt. What's on your mind, if any?"

"This story!" Timothy exclaimed. "This story you wrote! This story on the front page!"

"What about it?"

"What about it!" Timothy gasped. "You told me . . . public interest . . . don't worry . . . after what I told you . . . you told me . . ."

"You're not making sense, Hoppitt," said Harry coldly. "But then I never knew a rabbit who did. If you have anything to say to me, say it quickly. This is a busy day for me."

"And a fine sort of business you're up to!" said Timothy. "You know perfectly well that there's no lion in the woods!"

Harry looked straight into Timothy's eyes, in an unbearably calm and superior manner, and said:

"I know that you told me there isn't."

"What—"

"Then I read those notes you gave me, and I began

to take a different view. You know, Hoppitt, that's the difference between a real reporter like me and a beginner like you. You look no further than the facts; I look for the meaning behind the facts."

"Facts!" said Timothy indignantly. "What facts? The whole thing's a fraud!"

"Come, now, Hoppitt," Harry said, "that's a pretty reckless charge, isn't it? And even if it should happen to be a fraud, who's responsible for it? Eh?

"You told Mr. Reynard—"

"I told him one story. You told him another. He knew which of us to believe."

"What did you tell him? When we came back here yesterday, what did you say to him?"

"That you found the assignment was too big for you to handle, and that you didn't know what to do next, and that you came to me for help. He has no hard feelings against you. Of course, he might have if he saw that you wanted to get the *Daily Blade* in trouble."

Just then Red Reynard charged out of his office in a frenzy of pride and excitement.

"Harry!" he shouted. "Harry! Get over to City Hall right away!"

"City Hall?" said Harry.

"Yes! The Mayor just called me. He's accepted your offer!"

"Oh, has he?" said Harry coolly. "Well, I must say he took his time about it. Still, better late than never."

He got up, yawned, brushed himself.

"What offer?" Timothy asked suspiciously.

Harry smiled.

"I don't know that it's any of your business, Hoppitt," he said, "but I suggested to the Mayor that he appoint a committee to look for ways and means of driving these dangerous lions out of our woods, and I offered to serve as chairman of such a committee."

"It's a great honor for the paper, Harry," said Red Reynard. "And if your committee gets rid of the lions, you'll be the greatest hero Forest Park ever had."

"Oh, I'm not looking for glory," said Harry modestly. "Just doing a job in the public interest. You'll send a photographer over, of course?"

"Of course!" said Red Reynard.

"As for getting rid of the lions," said Harry, sliding a sly glance at Timothy, "I've an idea that won't be as difficult as it might seem to be. In fact, I think I'll tell the Mayor that he won't need a committee, after all. I'd rather handle the whole affair myself."

And Harry Fox swaggered away, leaving Red Reynard speechless with admiration and Timothy Hoppitt just plain speechless.

6 "Wondering Where the Truth Has Gone to"

IN THE DAYS that followed, Harry Fox did indeed prove that he could handle the whole affair himself. And if he was not looking for glory, he certainly seemed to have no objection when glory looked for him.

Each morning the *Daily Blade's* headlines were as big and black as ever, but now Harry Fox's name was in them, not under them:

FOX APPOINTED TO HEAD COMMITTEE TO FIGHT LION DANGER

FOX SAYS COMMITTEE UNNECESSARY; WILL DO JOB SINGLE-HANDED

MAYOR PRAISES FOX'S BRAVERY; ASKS ALL CITIZENS TO COOPERATE

FOX SEES VICTORY SURE IN CRUSADE AGAINST LIONS: "TAKE NO CHANCES"

NEW WARNING FROM HARRY FOX; SEVERAL
MORE LIONS MAY BE IN THE WOODS

So that he might have time and freedom to do his great work, Harry had been given a leave of absence (with pay) from the *Daily Blade.* Red Reynard, refusing to trust such tremendous news to lesser hands, was writing the stories himself.

Reading these stories, Timothy Hoppitt felt more helpless every day. This lion business had become like a snowball rolling downhill. Nothing could prevent it from growing bigger and bigger unless Harry Fox himself should call a halt, in order to collect his reward from a grateful forest.

One morning, as Timothy sat at his desk in a kind of trance (he had fallen into it while reading the latest headline: FOX OFFERS CHALLENGE; SAYS HE WILL TRY FOR PERSONAL MEETING WITH LIONS), Grabble Brown stopped to chat. Looking over Timothy's shoulder, Grabble said gruffly:

"Well, I guess it's time to take back what I used to say about Harry."

"Hm?" said Timothy.

"You know," Grabble said. "About not liking him and not trusting him. It just shows you can't judge by appearances. Now I would never have given that fox credit for being as brave as he is."

"Brave?" Timothy said, with a bitter little laugh.

"That's the word, isn't it?" said Grabble, giving Timothy a rather peculiar look. "I'm a pretty big and tough customer, if I do say so myself, but I wouldn't dare to meet one lion by myself, let alone three or four."

Timothy threw the paper down.

"You wouldn't mind meeting three thousand and sixty lions by yourself," he said, "and neither would I, if they were imaginary ones."

"Imaginary ones?" said Grabble. "Are you trying to say that—?"

"Of course!" Timothy replied. "There aren't any real lions in the woods. There never were. It started as a mistake, and it's turned into a terrible hoax."

"Timothy!" said Grabble, in a stern but friendly voice. "I think a lot of you, and always have, and I was just as upset . . . well, almost as upset as you were when Harry got the job that you should have had. But do you think it's right to carry a grudge so long, and spread rumors like this about someone who's risking his life for all of us?"

"But, Grabble!" Timothy protested. "This isn't a rumor, and I'm not carrying a grudge. It's only that—"

"Sportsmanship, Timothy," said Grabble, putting a heavy paw on Timothy's shoulder. "You have to be a good sport!"

And he lumbered away. Timothy thought that this was the saddest moment of his whole life. He would find that it wasn't.

Next day, when Timothy came to work, the office was in a fine buzz of excitement. At the door, the old porcupine exclaimed:

"He's going to do it! He's going to do it!"

"Who's going to do what?" said Timothy.

"Harry!" said the porcupine. "Harry's going to meet those lions! He'll show them who's boss! Oh, if I were young again!" And he rattled his quills in a menacing manner.

In the newsroom, a group of reporters had gathered around Roberta Robin's desk and, as he went by, Timothy heard Roberta trill:

"Meet! Meet! He's going to meet them! What a feat!"

When he reached his own desk, and looked at the newspaper, the headline read:

LIONS ASK FOR SECRET MEETING;

HARRY FOX SAYS "YES"

Timothy read it through.

The lions (there were, it seemed, three of them) had sent a messenger to Harry Fox. The messenger had come in the dead of night (of course) and no one had seen him except Harry (naturally) and the message had not been in writing (certainly not!). The lions accepted Harry's challenge to a personal meeting (so Harry said the messenger said), but the meeting would have to be a secret one (it would have to be!) in the loneliest part of the forest (Harry would see to that!).

The meeting was to take place in Shadow Valley this afternoon, although Mayor O'Possum had warned Harry that it might be a trap. The Mayor had offered to send along a heavy escort of police, but Harry had refused. "This is my job," the courageous Harry had said, "and I will carry it through alone!"

More than this, Harry had asked the Mayor to set a police guard at all entrances to the Valley to keep everybody out, and he had hired a squadron of ugly hawks to sweep through the skies to see that no inquisitive bird tried to get through.

"Harry seems to have thought of everything," said Willie Gray.

Timothy looked up at his friend.

"They're talking of running him for Mayor at the next election," Willie continued. Then, pointing to the headline: "That is, if he's still alive."

"Mayor!" Timothy murmured. "Oh, no, they can't!"

"Why not?" said Willie. "He's a very popular fellow already, and if he does what he's promised to do . . . if he gets rid of these lions—"

"Oh," said Timothy, "he'll do that all right. There's no question about it."

"Well, then—" Willie began.

Timothy took hold of Willie's sleeve.

"Willie," he said, "I've always told you the truth, haven't I?"

"Why, yes, Timothy," said Willie, in a puzzled tone. "Of course you have."

"And you know that I'd never tell you anything that wasn't true, don't you?"

"I'm sure of it."

"Well, I'm going to tell you something now that you'll find hard to believe. At least, everyone else has, and I expect you will, too. But it's the truth, Willie, even though things have gone so far now that I sometimes find myself wondering where the truth has gone to."

"What's the matter, Timothy? You look very pale."

"There's a reason."

And Timothy told him.

When the story was finished, Willie looked thoughtful but Timothy was happy to see that he didn't look as though he disbelieved.

"You mean there are no lions at all?" Willie said. "There never were any lions?"

"Never."

"And Harry knows it?"

"Certainly!" said Timothy warmly. "And that's why he's doing all this . . . all this flimflam! Shadow Valley! Secret meeting! You know what's going to happen, don't you? He's going to pretend that he's met the lions, and he'll pretend that he talked big to them, and then . . . all of a sudden, there won't be any lions!"

"There'll just be Harry," Willie Gray nodded. "Harry, the hero of Forest Park, and later . . . His Honor Harry the Mayor!"

"Isn't it terrible?" said Timothy. "How could anybody do such a thing?"

Willie Gray scratched his chin.

"Well, I don't know, Timothy," he said slowly. "Of course I don't approve of what Harry's doing. I agree that it certainly isn't altogether honest. But Harry's shrewd . . . he's clever . . . you've got to admit that he's using his brain to get ahead."

Timothy stared for a moment at his best friend, as if he couldn't believe his ears. Then he got up and swiftly walked away, with tears gathering in his eyes. Willie was still saying something, but Timothy didn't hear him. This, he knew, was really the saddest moment of his whole life.

He knew, too, that something, somehow, would have to be done to expose Harry Fox, and that now was the time.

Now . . . or never.

7

"Be Brave!
Be Resolute
Be Careful!"

EXPOSING HARRY FOX was easier said than done. Timothy considered one idea after another, all unworkable.

He would have to slip past the guards (he thought he knew how) and follow Harry into the dark and lonesome depths of Shadow Valley. But, there should be another witness, because his own story might not be believed. Who could he get to go with him? It seemed that everyone he knew lived in hero worship of Harry Fox or in fear of the lions, or both, and he couldn't very well ask someone he didn't know. A stranger might

spoil the show by giving Timothy's plan away before he
. had a chance to put it into effect.

Another witness. Where could he find another witness? Timothy looked up and blinked as the sun suddenly came from behind a cloud. The sun would be a
wonderful witness. The sun saw everything.

Then Timothy's mind came out from behind a cloud,
too. The sun would be going along, and with the sun's
help he could take pictures. A camera! There was his
other witness!

But would people believe the camera's story? Harry
would say the pictures were taken at another time in
some other place, and how could Timothy prove other-
wise? He couldn't, not with an ordinary camera. Wait,
though! Suppose it wasn't an ordinary camera? Suppose
it was a movie camera? He would have to rent one, and
the store would keep a record of the date of rental, and
if he had the film processed as soon as he returned, no
question could be raised about the day on which he
took it!

Timothy put the first part of his plan into action
at once. He rented a movie camera. Then came the

second part: a trip to the *Daily Blade's* library, where he spent half an hour studying maps of Shadow Valley and of the countryside around it.

A medium-sized crowd (of which Timothy was a part) had gathered at City Hall at two o'clock, and cheered (all except Timothy) when Harry Fox came out, accompanied by Mayor John J. O'Possum.

The Mayor, a stout little gray creature, could never resist the temptation to make a speech whenever he saw more than two persons in front of him. He started one now, but was cut short when Harry pointed at his wrist watch and said something in a low voice. The Mayor nodded, raised his arm as a signal, and a parade began to move down Buttercup Boulevard.

First in line were a dozen of Forest Park's finest police bears, strong, dependable, in the full vigor of their youth (the others were already on patrol duty, guarding the ways that led to Shadow Valley). Then, arm in arm, walked Harry Fox and the Mayor, talking together in a very serious manner. Then came the twenty members of the Forest Park City Council (a varied lot among whom a field mouse was the smallest, a beaver was the

oldest, and a weasel was the shiftiest). Then came the crowd, and Timothy.

At Bramble Pass, just this side of Shadow Valley, the parade halted. The Mayor started to make another speech, but Harry again politely interrupted, and the Mayor had to be content with shaking Harry's paw in a strenuous way and saying, "Good luck! Be brave! Be resolute! Be careful!" Then, as the crowd set up another cheer (without Timothy's voice), Harry Fox slid away into the thick tangles of Bramble Pass.

Now that the hero had left them, the crowd, the Council, and even the Mayor began to feel nervous. A thin red squirrel, trembling beside Timothy, said in a hoarse whisper:

"Maybe it *is* a trap! Maybe the lions just wanted to get Harry out of the way so they could pounce on us!"

This thought seemed to be occurring to a good many persons, because the crowd was quickly and quietly beginning to move away.

Timothy, carrying his rented movie camera, moved away too.

The maps at the newspaper library had shown a number of now-deserted tunnels that followed a winding underground course from this part of the forest to Shadow Valley, but Timothy found that locating their entrances on a piece of parchment was much easier than locating them in the ground. He spotted one at last, but a police bear stood directly in front of it. The bear kept his stern and silent stare fixed on Timothy until he had hopped by.

There should have been one near Ragged Oak Road, but a tree had fallen and blocked it up.

There should have been another near Wild Rose Terrace, but although Timothy sniffed and scratched in a dozen places, he could not find it.

As he stopped to catch his breath, he held it instead. A huge black shadow seemed to surround him, and from the corner of his eye he saw a yellow claw descending.

With incredible speed he shot forward to escape the hawk, and the ground broke open beneath him!

He lay for a moment in the dusty darkness where he had fallen, heard the hawk's harsh scream of baffled rage, heard answering cries from a distance. Then, realizing that he was unhurt and out of danger, he crouched and crawled along the narrow tunnel.

If the map was right, he should before long come to the other end of the tunnel, where he could look out into Shadow Valley. Then, if his luck held and he found Harry . . .

There were side branches that had not appeared on the map, but Timothy was not tempted to take any of them. However, when he had been moving forward in a straight line for what seemed an endless time, he came to a puzzle that stopped him in his tracks.

The tunnel itself divided in two.

This had not appeared on the map, either. Which tunnel should Timothy follow now? The one on the left? Or the one on the right? He tried to scratch his ear, but there wasn't room. Well, he had to go one way or the other. Quite probably both tunnels ended at last in Shadow Valley.

He went to the right.

The farther he went, the more uneasy he felt about the choice he had made. The turns and twists in this underground passageway were so many and so abrupt that he half expected to swing around one corner just in time to see himself disappearing around another. He kept on, however, without hesitation. It was too late to turn back now, and he could only hope that the creature who had made this tunnel had not done it as a practical joke.

His nose twitched. From somewhere up ahead had come the gentlest whiff of fresh air. As he went around another bend—it must have been the fifty-fifth, at least —he saw a pinpoint of light. He scratched along with more speed.

At the tunnel's end he came out into sunshine so bright that his eyes hurt and he had to close them. When he opened them, to see where he was . . .

He groaned.

Just ahead of him, tall and forbidding, loomed Eagle Rock. To the right was a field that bordered Highway 47. To the left, the woods began sloping up a steep hill. He was still on the wrong side of Shadow Valley, and miles farther from it than he had been when he started.

Well, his plan was ruined beyond hope of repair. In the time that would take him back to the division in the tunnel, and along the left branch, and into Shadow

Valley, Harry Fox would have been able to get rid of any number of make-believe lions and return in triumph to Forest Park.

Timothy was hot. He was hopeless. He was also hungry. So he went down into the field and started to eat.

He couldn't say that he enjoyed the meal. Disappointment made the most luscious grass and clover seem tasteless. But if he didn't relish the food, he relished even less being interrupted in his eating, and that is what happened.

Somewhere behind him he heard a high screeching sound, then a crash of metal, then a shouting of men. His mouth was full, but he stopped chewing and stayed stock-still. He had always found this the safest thing to do when threatened by danger, unless that danger swooped from the sky.

The most comforting thing about Timothy's present position was that he was well hidden in the high grass. The most discomforting thing—and annoying as well —was that the height of the grass prevented him from seeing what was going on. He could only guess from the noises that he heard, and none of the noises was reassuring. Least of all the newest noise: a heavy snuffling sound that seemed to come from only a short distance away.

He had never heard anything like it, he never wanted to hear anything like it again, but he would like to know what was making it. The trouble was, if he made the slightest move to see what it was, what it was would undoubtedly see him. This was a time, Timothy felt, when caution was a better guide than curiosity.

So he waited without stirring, without chewing, until the snuffling sound slowly moved away and, at last, could not be heard any more. Men were still shouting, but their voices were distant and Timothy could sense no danger from them.

With a quick chew and gulp he finished his mouthful of grass and hopped back to the entrance of the tunnel, where he could take a wide view of the country.

The field that he had just left was empty. Beyond it there appeared to be a great flurry of men and machines on Highway 47, but this was so far away that Timothy could not make out what was going on. On the hill to the left, where the woods began, something was moving . . .

Something large.

Something brown.

Something stealthy.

A lion! A real lion! A lion was entering the woods! Jungle terror, somewhat late but still terrible, had come to Forest Park!

8

"His Honor the Mayor Will See You"

SMALL GROUPS of happy and excited persons were leaving the green in front of City Hall when Timothy, aching and out of breath, came loping up. One of them shouted something to him, but he was so tired and so intent upon his errand that he didn't hear the words.

He went into City Hall and hurried down the long rocky corridor to the door with the Mayor's name on it. He opened the door, and a snappish raccoon who was Mayor O'Possum's secretary glanced up from his paper work and said:

"Yes, yes? Who are you? What's your business here?"

"I have to—to see the Mayor!" Timothy panted. "Very —very important!"

"His Honor the Mayor is extremely busy," said the raccoon. "Can't be disturbed. Come back tomorrow."

"Tomorrow may be too late!" said Timothy. "I must see him now! It's urgent!"

The raccoon was so irritated that he broke a pencil in two.

"I said, come back tomorrow!" he exclaimed. "If you have a complaint, put it down in writing and bring it tomorrow, and I'll see that His Honor the Mayor has it brought to his attention."

"It isn't a complaint—" said Timothy.

"All right," said the raccoon. "So you want a job. Make your application in writing and bring three copies with you tomorrow, and I'll see that His Honor the Mayor —"

"I don't want a job!" Timothy said. "I just have to see the Mayor now!"

The raccoon's beady eyes looked Timothy up and down. "You don't have a complaint and you don't want a job," he said. "Then you can't have any honest reason for wanting to see His Honor the Mayor. Besides, there's a wild look in your eyes that I don't like."

"There'd be a wild look in yours," said Timothy, "if you'd seen what I've seen!"

The raccoon moved back a few steps nervously.

"We don't want to have any trouble, do we?" he said. "If you don't go quietly, I'll have to call the police, won't I?"

"Trouble!" said Timothy. "Trouble! There's a lion in the woods! That means real trouble! I tell you, I must see the Mayor—"

The raccoon looked relieved, and even managed a moderately good-humored chuckle.

"I guess you haven't heard the news, have you?" he said. "We've taken care of that situation. There aren't any lions in the woods any more. We've driven them away. Harry Fox, that is, working for us in the city government—"

"I have later news than that," said Timothy. "Harry Fox didn't drive them all away. There's still one left over."

The raccoon's eyes widened. He pulled thoughtfully at his chin.

"If what you say is true," he said, "then His Honor the Mayor will certainly want to know about it. What did you say your name was?"

"I'm Hoppitt, of the *Daily Blade,*" said Timothy.

"A reporter!" the raccoon exclaimed. "Why didn't you say so? And you've seen another lion? Just a moment, please."

He disappeared rapidly into the Mayor's office. Timothy heard a murmur of voices, and then the raccoon returned.

"Go right in," he said. "His Honor the Mayor will see you."

"Thank you," said Timothy, and went right in.

The Mayor was hanging by his tail from a tree root that ran the length of the ceiling. He gave Timothy a genial wave with one paw; the other was clutching a telephone.

"Make yourself comfortable," he said. "I'll be down with you soon. Official business, you know. I'm dictating a proclamation."

"Your Honor," said Timothy, "I—"

"And whereas," said the Mayor into the telephone, "a terrible danger has been removed from our fair forest, and whereas the removal of this danger has been due to the untiring efforts and the unbelievable courage of one individual, namely Harry Fox—"

"The danger," said Timothy, "it hasn't been removed. It's still—"

"Be with you in a moment, young fellow," the Mayor said, with another wave of his paw. "Poppitt, I think you said your name was? Always glad to meet a newspaperman. This won't take long . . . Let's see . . . Ready? Now, therefore, I, John J. O'Possum, Mayor of Forest Park, do hereby proclaim tomorrow, Tuesday, July 24, a public holiday in honor of Harry Fox, and do also proclaim that said day shall be known as Harry Fox Day. Furthermore, I do request that all citizens of Forest Park gather together at two o'clock in the afternoon of said day in Mayflower Meadow—"

"Oh, no!" Timothy burst out. "If everyone's gathered together in one place, they'll all be in dreadful danger! There's a lion—"

"Shhhhh!" said the Major, showing some vexation. "You really mustn't interrupt me, young fellow! Disturbs my thinking, don't you see? And I have to think clearly when it's official business. . . . Mayflower Meadow," he said into the telephone. "You have that? Good.

In Mayflower Meadow to witness the presentation to said Harry Fox of the highest award that it is in the power of Forest Park to bestow, namely, the Golden Medal of Merit, and to pay tribute, by their presence, to the wisdom and bravery of said Harry Fox. That's all. See that it gets to the newspaper, won't you? All right. Good-by!"

He dropped the telephone to his desk and dropped himself into the chair behind his desk, where he sat smiling pleasantly at Timothy.

"Now then!" he said. "Sorry to keep you waiting, young fellow. My secretary said something about an iron?"

"No, Your Honor," said Timothy. "It's about a lion. I just saw a lion going into the woods near Highway 47."

"Oh, my, no, no!" said Mayor O'Possum. "That was several days ago."

"But this was a real lion!"

"There were three lions," said the Mayor, "but they've gone now. Harry Fox met them just a little while ago this very afternoon, and he told them that if they didn't get out and stay out he'd give them a beating they wouldn't care to remember and then he'd throw them out himself. And do you know what they did?"

"I suppose they vanished into thin air," said Timothy dryly. "The same thin air they came from."

"Eh? No, not at first," said the Mayor. "They had the

impudence to start to talk back. But Harry reached out and boxed the ears of one of them so soundly that they all tucked their tails between their legs and ran out of the woods!"

"But another one ran in," said Timothy. "Don't you understand, sir? I've just seen a lion."

"Might have been a dream?" the Mayor suggested.

"I was wide awake."

"Something you ate, perhaps?"

"Something that might eat me, or any of us!"

"The sun's been very hot, today. Might have affected your mind?"

"No, Your Honor. There's a live lion loose in Forest Park!"

Mayor O'Possum sighed.

"This is really very troublesome," he said, reaching for the telephone again. "Just when everything was going along so nicely, too. . . . Hello, is this Harry Fox's office? . . . Is Harry there? . . . Harry, this is John J. There's a rabbit come to see me. Name of Popover. Says he works for the *Daily Blade*. Says he's just seen another lion go-

ing into the woods from Highway 47. . . . What? . . .
Yes. . . . Oh, he is? . . . Oh, he does? . . . I see. Thank
you, Harry. Sorry to bother you when you've had such a
busy day, but of course I wanted to find out. . . . You'll
have dinner at the house tonight, won't you, with Mrs.
O'Possum and me? . . . Fine! See you then!"

He hung up, and sent a searching look at Timothy.

"Have you any proof that you've seen a lion?" he de-
manded.

With a sinking feeling, Timothy realized that, in the
excitement of the moment, he had forgotten that he had
a movie camera. There was no proof.

"No, sir," he said. "No actual proof, but—"

"See here, Popover!" Mayor O'Possum said. "I suspected from the minute you came into this office that
you were up to something. Now I know it! Harry Fox
says that he's had trouble with you and your imaginary
lions before."

"Me and my—!"

"Now, not another word! You just get out of this
building as fast as you can! You ought to be ashamed of
yourself. Trying to make a name for yourself by tarnish-

ing the reputation of a real hero like Harry Fox! I tell you if I owned the newspaper you wouldn't work on it another day. No, sir! Not another day! That's all!"

And Mayor O'Possum pointed to the door.

9

"A Stranger
in These Parts"

HARRY FOX DAY dawned fair and hot, and from the earliest hours of the morning the people of Forest Park started to gather in the big meadow where all important games and celebrations were held.

From his home, Timothy Hoppitt watched them streaming by: chattering gangs of chipmunks and squirrels, whole families of heavy-set bears, deer moving with timid grace, an old porcupine walking alone and mumbling to himself, a skulk of foxes cheering their heads off.

At first, Timothy had thought that he would not go, not because of the danger that he, and he alone, knew might threaten the throng, but because he didn't think he could stand listening to the undeserved praises that would be showered on Harry Fox. Then, late in the morning, he changed his mind. If he could find a place somewhere close to the speakers' platform and keep his eyes fixed in an accusing stare at Harry Fox, maybe Harry's conscience would begin to trouble him. Even in the likelier case that Harry didn't have a conscience, at least he would realize that there was one person in the great crowd who was not there to pay tribute to Harry's wisdom and bravery.

So, when noon came around, Timothy Hoppitt left his home and headed for Mayflower Meadow. When he

arrived there, he wriggled his way through the crowd and, by the greatest good luck, found an open space at the very foot of the platform in the middle of the meadow.

The Mayor and the City Council and Harry Fox had not yet appeared on the scene, but the platform was occupied by Humphrey Humpapump's Band (made up of small tree toads who piped and huge bullfrogs who boomed) and a number of speakers and singers who took turns trying to ·entertain the audience until it should be time for the big event of the afternoon. Their efforts could not be called highly successful, for the audience itself kept up such a grunting and cheeping, and growling and chirping, and laughing and singing, and scolding and cheering, that no one who was more than three feet away from the platform could hear what was going on up there at all.

At ten minutes before two o'clock the official party arrived, making its way slowly through the throng, which went wild with enthusiasm and became wilder when the Mayor and Harry Fox mounted to the platform and waved.

The band struck up a lively march: "Once Around the Oak Tree, Twice Around the Pine."

Timothy Hoppitt stared at Harry, but Harry didn't notice him.

The music stopped. The Mayor stepped forward, held up his paw, cleared his throat, and commenced to speak. The audience became quiet, except for a couple of baby bears who were cuffing each other in play. When their father cuffed them they grinned and became quiet too.

Mayor O'Possum spoke, as usual, in a loud and droning voice, and his speech, as usual, seemed to go on and on and round and about and back and forth. But the crowd listened patiently and with growing excitement because it knew that the big moment was on its way.

And at last the big moment came!

"Harry Fox!" said the Mayor, and put his arm around Harry, and they both waved again, and the cheering rose and roared again.

"Harry Fox," said the Mayor, reaching out for something that a Council member handed him, something that gleamed and glittered in the afternoon sun, "it is my great pleasure to salute you for your tremendous courage

in delivering Forest Park from the . . . er . . . tremendous danger it has faced!"

At these words, Harry Fox bowed his head modestly and, as he did so, caught Timothy Hoppitt's stare. His expression did not change much, but he blinked and for the fraction of a second a small mocking smile played around his mouth.

"Harry Fox," said the Mayor, "we are proud of you and you have earned our undying and . . . er . . . tremendous gratitude . . ."

"Hurray!" shouted the crowd in the meadow.

"Hurray!" shouted Mr. Griswold Grunter.

Mr. Grunter had been so busy chucking wood all morning that he had not been able to get to the celebration until after it had started, and by that time the only place he could find was away at the edge of Mayflower Meadow, where the woods began. He couldn't hear all that was being said, he couldn't see anything that was being done on the platform, but he cheered when everyone else did and he was having a fine time.

"Hurray!" he shouted.

"I ask your pardon, sir," said a voice beside him, a deep and very distinguished voice.

"Granted," said Mr. Grunter, without looking around.

"May I make so bold as to inquire —"

"Shhhh!" said Mr. Grunter impatiently, straining his ears to make out what Mayor O'Possum was saying.

"We can never fully repay you," said the Mayor, "for your . . . er . . . tremendous public service, and what we are doing today is only a small token . . . a very small token . . . of what we should like to do! This is a day that Forest Park will not soon forget, and Forest Park will never forget the fox who made this day possible!"

"Hurray!" shouted the crowd in the meadow.

"Hurray!" shouted Mr. Grunter when he heard the others doing it.

Abruptly the thought crossed his mind that the voice which had begged his pardon a moment ago, and which had interrupted him when he was trying to hear the Mayor, was now silent, and that at no time had he heard this particular voice raised in a cheer. Mr. Grunter turned and peered with suspicious eyes at the owner of the voice.

"I don't recollect seeing you around here before," he said. "Likely you're a stranger in these parts?"

"Yes, I am."

"Hmmmm!" said Mr. Grunter. "Then I guess you don't know what's been going on?"

"No, I don't, as a matter of fact. But what I wanted to ask you—"

"Wellsirree, sir!" Mr. Grunter persisted. "We've had just about the most exciting old time you could think of! Yessirree, bob! We had three lions roaming around these woods."

The stranger looked interested.

"Oh?" he said. "Really? You mean, there are three other lions nearby?"

"Not any more there aren't," said Mr. Grunter. "This

fellow Harry Fox, he . . ." Mr. Grunter stopped suddenly, stared at his neighbor, and seemed to be having some difficulty in breathing. "Other lions?" he said. "Other? Are you a—?"

"Am I a what?"

"A-a-a-a . . ." said Mr. Grunter, beginning to back away. "A . . . a . . . lion?"

"Yes," said the lion. "Oh, but how impolite of me! Allow me to introduce myself."

And he held out his paw.

"A LION!" shouted Mr. Grunter, and took off as fast as his legs would carry him. He bumped into a weasel, who sneered:

"Why don't you watch where you're going?"

"A LION!" yelled Mr. Grunter, pointing behind him. The weasel looked.

"A LION!" shrieked the weasel, and slithered away with the speed of a shadow.

"A LION!" cried all the creatures nearby, and ran. The cry commenced to spread.

In the middle of a long sentence, Mayor John J. O'Possum became aware that a disturbance of some kind was taking place at one side of the meadow. He kept on talking, hoping that the trouble would fade away. It didn't. The disturbance seemed to be growing. Now he could see that he was losing a good part of his audience. Some were running into the woods, some were flying into the air, some were burrowing into the ground. They were shouting, too, and the Mayor attempted the rather difficult trick of trying to hear what they were saying at the same time that he was trying to hear what *he* was saying.

"A LION! A LION!"

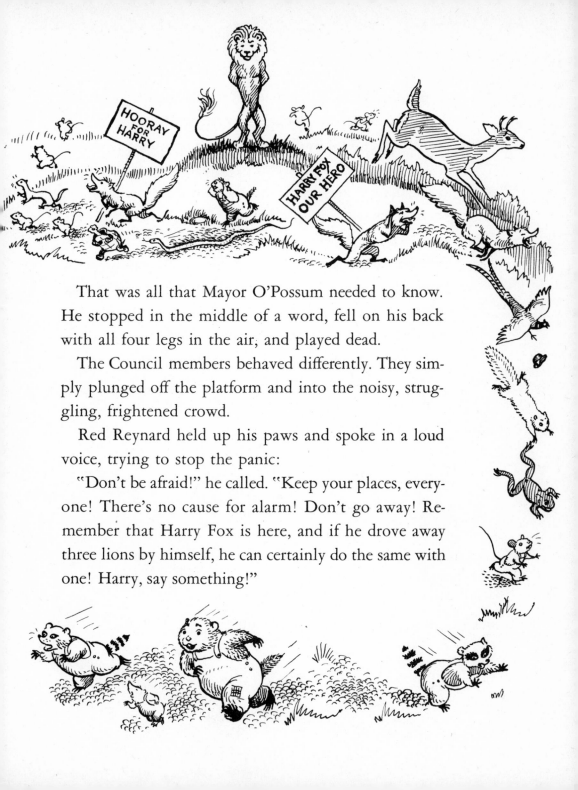

That was all that Mayor O'Possum needed to know. He stopped in the middle of a word, fell on his back with all four legs in the air, and played dead.

The Council members behaved differently. They simply plunged off the platform and into the noisy, struggling, frightened crowd.

Red Reynard held up his paws and spoke in a loud voice, trying to stop the panic:

"Don't be afraid!" he called. "Keep your places, everyone! There's no cause for alarm! Don't go away! Remember that Harry Fox is here, and if he drove away three lions by himself, he can certainly do the same with one! Harry, say something!"

"Shut up, you old fool!" snarled Harry Fox. "This is a real lion! Get out of my way!"

And he pushed Red Reynard aside and jumped down and ran. The newspaper publisher was stunned for a moment. Then, realizing how he had been tricked, he showed his teeth angrily and set off in pursuit of Harry.

Mayflower Meadow, which had taken a whole morning and part of the afternoon to fill, was emptied in less than ten minutes. Almost emptied, that is. Three figures remained: the motionless Mayor, Timothy Hoppitt, and the lion, who now trotted toward them.

10

"D'You Know What This Young Fellow Did?"

WHEN TIMOTHY HOPPITT heard what Harry Fox said, and saw what Harry Fox did, he started to chuckle, and then he started to laugh, and he laughed so hard and so long that tears came into his eyes. When he brushed them away with his paw, and looked around, he saw that the crowd had vanished and that the lion was standing not half a yard away.

Still he couldn't keep himself from giggling, and the sound seemed to displease the lion, who growled deep in the throat and glared at him.

"Are you laughing at me?" said the lion.

Timothy shook his head.

"No," he said. "I heard a little joke a while ago, and it just occurred to me how funny it really was."

"I see," said the lion. "That's all right, then. I met a very rude and impolite creature over there, and I thought you might be another one, that's all. Then everyone started to call my name, and I was prepared to say a few words in response, and all of a sudden everyone had gone. Is that the way you usually treat strangers in your country?"

"We don't often have strangers of your sort visit us, you know," said Timothy.

"It's easy to see that," said the lion. "But you, at least, seem to behave in a reasonable and courteous manner. May I have the honor of knowing to whom I speak?"

"Oh," said Timothy. "My name is Hoppitt. Timothy Hoppitt. I'm a reporter for the *Daily Blade.*"

The lion raised his eyebrows and cocked his head on

one side and looked down at Timothy with respect.

"A reporter?" he said. "You mean you work for a newspaper? Ah, then, no doubt you'd like an interview with me. I daresay you don't often have the chance to write about lions in your newspaper, do you?"

"Well . . ." said Timothy, not quite sure of what to say.

"It would have to be very brief, I'm afraid," said the lion, "because I'm rather pressed for time. Born in South Africa, you know, and all that. Traveled to Europe at an early age, featured artist with the Kollmann Circus in Vienna. Played before the crowned heads, and so forth. Later made many successful appearances in the United States of America. . . . Are you putting all this down?"

"I shan't forget a word of it," said Timothy truthfully.

"Good!" said the lion. "Ah, yes! Unmarried. Favorite color: red. Favorite flower: chrysanthemum. Favorite trick: doing the double somersault. Perhaps you'd like to see that?"

"Indeed I would!" said Timothy. "Would you perform it for me, please?"

"Oh, no!" the lion said in a shocked tone. "I couldn't

possibly perform it when someone asks as nicely as that. You see," he went on proudly, "I've been trained to obey commands. You must speak to me sharply!"

"Sharply?" Timothy's voice was doubtful.

"As sharply as you can," said the lion. "I shall close my eyes and pretend that you're my trainer. Of course, you don't have a whip and so you can't crack it, but I shall just have to imagine. Are you ready?"

He closed his eyes.

Timothy took a deep breath and then, in as loud a voice as he could manage, he exclaimed:

"Double somersault, you, and be quick about it!"

The lion smiled happily, and rolled off in a double somersault that was quite the most astonishing sight Timothy had ever seen. Then the beast got up, brushed the dirt and the grass from his coat, and came trotting back.

"I hope you liked it?" he asked.

"It was wonderful," said Timothy.

"Oh, nothing to what I can do in the circus ring," said the lion, "when my trainer orders me to. You don't have a trainer, I suppose?"

"No."

"You don't know what you're missing," said the lion. And then, with sudden remembrance: "That reminds me! I wanted to ask, do you know how I can find my way back to Highway 47? I'm completely turned about in this strange country."

"Why, yes," said Timothy. "It's about a mile from here, north-northwest. You go through that clump of trees over there, and you'll find a path that will lead you right out to the highway."

"I can't tell you how grateful I am!" said the lion. "You see, my cage fell off a truck on the highway yesterday, and the door broke open, and I was so confused that I ran into the woods and got lost."

"Oh?"

"Yes, and it was so stupid of me, because the last thing in the world I want to do is leave the circus. They arrange everything for you there, you know. You don't have to bother yourself with anything except, of course, doing what they tell you to do. Free meals, a nice cozy cage . . . I can't wait to get back!"

"You really like that kind of life?" asked Timothy.

"Like it!" said the lion. "I wouldn't be able to live without it! Through those trees, you said?"

"That's right."

"Thank you!" said the lion. "Thank you ever so much!" He started off, and then turned. "Oh, by the way," he called, "when you write your story, be sure to get my first name right."

"What is your first name?" said Timothy.

"It's Benedick," said the lion. "Unusual, perhaps, but I think it's rather distinctive. Benedick. With a *k*, not a *t*. A *k*, like the chap in Shakespeare's *Much Ado About Nothing.* Good-by!"

"Good-by!" said Timothy.

The lion reached the clump of trees, waved, and disappeared into the forest.

"A *k,* not a *t,*" Timothy repeated softly to himself. "Like the chap in *Much Ado About Nothing!*" Then he started to chuckle, and then he started to laugh, and he laughed so hard and so long that tears came into his eyes, and when he brushed them away with his paws, and looked around, he saw that he was surrounded by Council members, and Red Reynard and Willie Gray and others from the *Daily Blade.* Beyond them, more and more of the crowd were coming back into the meadow.

"Are you all right, Timothy?" asked Willie Gray.

"Did he bite you?" asked Red Reynard.

"Does it hurt?" asked a Council member.

Mayor O'Possum came to life and pushed his way through the circle around Timothy.

"Bravest thing I ever saw in my life!" he said, tossing an arm around Timothy. "I couldn't hear everything, but I had one eye open, and just as that monster was about to open his jaws and devour this young fellow, d'you know what this young fellow did? He said 'Do a double

somersault, you, and be quick about it!' And then the lion knew who his master was, and he did a double somersault, you can bet! And then he came back, and this young fellow told him to get, and he got! Bravest thing I ever saw! I hereby proclaim that from this time forward Tuesday, July 24, be celebrated in Forest Park as a public holiday, and that it be known as . . . What did you say your name was, young fellow?"

"Popover," said Timothy, and then he giggled again, and said: "With a *k,* not a *t.*"

"Are you sure you're all right?" asked Red Reynard.

Later that afternoon, Timothy Hoppitt sat at his desk in the *Daily Blade* newsroom. He placed a clean sheet of paper in his typewriter, took a sip of the lemonade that Red Reynard had bought him, touched the Golden Medal of Merit that Mayor O'Possum had given him, waved the eager copy boys away and told them that he'd call them when he needed them, winked at Willie Gray, and tapped out on the typewriter keys:

MY MEETING WITH BENEDICK LION
By
The Blade's Star Reporter
TIMOTHY HOPPITT

"Timothy," said Willie Gray. "Weren't you scared?"

Timothy thought for a moment. Then he smiled.

"Yes," he said. "I certainly was, right at first. But then I saw how foolish it was."

"Foolish?"

"Because, tell me, Willie, why should anybody who's free be afraid of anybody who lives in a cage and likes it?"